To the 2020 pandemic:

Thank you for the time to
play, learn, love, craft, move,
appreciate, and reflect.

when the world stays inside

words by Mikey Woz
Pictures by Sara Panchaud

Now and then there are times
when the world must stay in.
It might be the rain,
or the snow, or the wind.

But sometimes it's because
we don't want to get sick.
And from inside we'll wonder,
how did it happen so quick?

when the world
stays inside...

we'll have time to get cuddly,
curled up on the couch
feeling cozy and lovely.

But that isn't all,
there's so MUCH we can do.
There's fun to be had,
and it's all up to you.

when the world
stays inside...

there's more time we can spend,
making forts for the picnics,
we'll have with our friends.

when the world stays inside...

we'll have more time to bake.

We'll make big giant cakes
and eat them all in a day.

And then we will share
our big giant cakes,
because sharing is caring.
Now, wouldn't you say?

we won't want to stand still,

when the world
stays inside...

we'll want to get moving
with some fun exercise.

we'll stretch and we'll run
and find new ways to play.
It feels better to dance
than sit the whole day away.

when the world
stays inside...

we can take time to learn.
There's knowledge to earn
when you have time to burn.

we can learn about people
in faraway lands,
or study every bone
that we have in our hands.

when the world
stays inside...

time can slow to a crawl.
But it's fun to build things
for no reason at all!

we can build boats and planes
and dream of wandering far.
we can go anywhere
from right where we are.

when the world
stays inside...

it's the most perfect chance
to sing all the songs that
make us smile and dance.

It doesn't matter if we know
how to carry a tune,
singing songs always
makes a fun afternoon.

when the world
stays inside...

we'll take the time to pretend.
The world has no limits
when we just use our heads.

when the world
stays inside...

we'll take time to say hi.
we'll reach out to loved ones,
no need for goodbyes.

when the world
stays inside...

we'll have plenty of time,
to tidy our homes and
make them sparkle and shine.

we can pick up our toys
and see the goldfish is fed.

we can clear all the cobwebs
from under our bed.

when the world
stays inside...

we'll have time to just draw.
we'll bring new friends to life
or just draw what we saw.

we'll draw rainbows and turtles
and tall purple giraffes.
And if we get bored of that,
we can start making crafts!

when the world
stays inside...

there's no reason to hide,
because the people who love us
are always nearby.

so while we wait for the day
we can go back outside,
let's try all the things
that we still haven't tried.

when we're wrinkly and grey
and we've lived our whole lives,
we will cherish that time
that the world stayed inside.

Made in the USA
Middletown, DE
04 August 2020